Tweeg Gets the Tweezles

This story shows the value of being a good neighbor,
and the importance of a positive attitude.

Story by:
Ken Forsse
Michelle Baron

Illustrated by:

Russell Hicks
Theresa Mazurek
Douglas McCarthy
Allyn Conley-Gorniak
Lorann Downer

Rivka
Fay Whitemountain
Suzanne Lewis
Lisa Souza

WORLDS OF WONDER™

Worlds of Wonder, Inc. is the exclusive licensee, manufacturer and distributor of the World of Teddy Ruxpin toys. "The World of Teddy Ruxpin" and "Teddy Ruxpin" are trademarks of Alchemy II, Inc., Chatsworth, CA. The symbol ✺•✺ and "Worlds of Wonder" are trademarks of Worlds of Wonder, Inc., Fremont, California.

Grubby® Newton Gimmick™ Princess Aruzia™ Leota™ Wooly What's-It™ Prince Arin™ Fobs®

Teddy

Hello there. How are you? Uh huh, and how are you feeling, Grubby?

Grubby

Oh…well, let me see. Yep, I feel great! Thank you.

Teddy

That's good.

Grubby

Why do ya ask?

Teddy

Oh, I was just thinking about the time that Tweeg was not feeling very well.

Grubby

Oh yeah, I remember that.